MINI...S

...RE
STARTS HERE ...

CUMBRIA

First published in Great Britain in 2009 by
Young Writers, Remus House, Coltsfoot Drive,
Peterborough, PE2 9JX
Tel (01733) 890066 Fax (01733) 313524
All Rights Reserved

© Copyright Contributors 2008
SB ISBN 978-1-84431-865-0

FOREWORD

Young Writers was established in 1990 with the aim of encouraging and nurturing writing skills in young people and giving them the opportunity to see their work in print. By helping them to become more confident and expand their creative skills, we hope our young writers will be encouraged to keep writing as they grow.

Secondary school pupils nationwide have been exercising their minds to create their very own short stories, using no more than fifty words, to be included here in our latest competition *The Adventure Starts Here...* .

The entries we received showed an impressive level of technical skill and imagination, an absorbing look into the eager minds of our future authors.

CONTENTS

THE MINI SAGAS

MATILDA

Matilda was adopted by horrible parents who treated her meanly. Her school teacher treated her badly. She loved school but not the teacher. Parents Mr and Mrs Werewood shouted at her for the worst things. Another teacher Mrs Hunny was lovely. Matilda's parents left. Matilda lived with Mrs Hunny.

JADE GREEN (12)
Caldew School, Carlisle

1

FLAT ANT

Me and Bob are twins. We go everywhere together
and we are ants. There was food left on a bench,
we went to get some and a human sat on Bob!
He said he was OK but he was not. He was really,
really flat, as flat as a pancake.

ALIX LANCASTER (12)

Caldew School, Carlisle

ELMO AND BIRDY

One hundred years ago there was an elephant called Elmo. Elmo lived on his own in a jungle, knowing that soon his time would come and he would die.
Whilst drinking at the river, a bird sat on his back.
Elmo and Birdy became friends and lived a happy life.

VICKI RICHARDS (12)

Caldew School, Carlisle

A TERRORIST'S LAST THOUGHT, MY TURN!

Crash! The charge went off.
'Go, go, go!' SAS Captain Price shouted.
They stormed into the house, night vision goggles on,
guns blazing.
'Floor clear,' Gaz said into his intercom.
'Moving to upper floors.'
A terrorist upstairs heard a burst of shots,
three men around him went down.
'My turn …'

ANANTA HANDLEY (12)
Caldew School, Carlisle

TRAPPED

Trapped, the boy was at a dead end; the gang advanced. What had he done to deserve this? A small, well-built chav came forward, he pulled out a large, sharp knife. He stabbed. The boy felt the cold blade inside him, he fell. It went black, the footsteps faded.

CALLUM DUGGAN (13)
Caldew School, Carlisle

CREATURE

There was once a princess who lived in a castle near the sea. One day she found an old wardrobe; she opened it and found an underground world. She went in and she found a mystical creature. It was pink and fluffy. She asked, 'Who are you?' It didn't reply!

LUCY TEMPLETON (12)

Caldew School, Carlisle

THE CUMBRIANS!

'How's fettle marra? Az garn owa yonda hill t'plough
yan field them Smiths bin larkin' abouwt
on halls land!'
'Soft townies! Yan atime townies stayed in town, not
in owa fields! Wasn't for us farmers, idiots would die!'
'Aye well, az garn to bash on field divent
plough itself lad.'

HELEN BROWN & MARTIN HALL (13)

Caldew School, Carlisle

7

HOW TO SPOT A WITCH

To spot a witch you need to be sneaky. Why?
They don't like children, they hate their smell.
They are bald but they wear a wig so their heads are
very itchy. They have blue tongues, great big claws,
no toes, colour-changing eyes. That's how you
spot a witch.

SOPHIE MCMILLAN (12)
Caldew School, Carlisle

MATILDA

'Nag! Nag!' her parents yelled, 'Do this, do that!'
She had no worries; she was special. She pointed her
finger and all her worries went.
She went to school and things were bad, until she got
adopted! Everything was good and she lived happily
ever after.

NICOLE DODD (12)

Caldew School, Carlisle

UNTITLED

Five golden tickets, one boy, one dream. As a young boy Charlie Bucket was poor, he had to work for minimum wage. But one day Charlie found a golden ticket and asked his grandad to come - he hadn't moved from his bed in ages - but Charlie followed his chocolate dream.

KEANU HOPE (12)

Caldew School, Carlisle

THE ATTIC TWINS

We moved to the house across the road. When we got there Mum told me to go explore and that's when I saw the twins. I asked them where they came from and they just looked at me. After three months I went back up and they were gone forever!

RAYANNE STRONG (12)

Caldew School, Carlisle

DEATH

He was running up the volcano. He got to the top
and there, floating above the volcano, a black box
with a green glow. It flew at him, knocked him off the
volcano. He fell, landed in a bush. The box opened
… in the glow there was a warlock.

MICHAEL FOSTER (12)

Caldew School, Carlisle

THE SECRET MAN

It all started when I woke up this morning.
We had just moved house yesterday so I was still
exploring the new house. I noticed an old shack at
the back of my garden. I went up to the door.
I went in and I saw an old man.
'Argh!'

LUCY JANE WILKINSON (12)

Caldew School, Carlisle

THE MAN WITH NO NAME

There was an old battered up Ferrari with him.
I opened the old door. It nearly fell off in my hand.
I sat down on the seat and the man flicked the
button. He said, 'Fasten your seat belts!'

TONY LOSH (12)
Caldew School, Carlisle

SUPER SALLY'S SHOPPING DAY

Sally was thirteen and was going into town by herself.
She had a phone to feel safe. Sally was walking into
town and came across some chavs, she walked faster.
They started to chase! Sally got into town;
the police came and gave the chavs an ASBO!

ROBYN SHEAD (13)

Caldew School, Carlisle

THE LONELY CAT

There was once a cat that was called Fluffy who lived
in a little old house all by himself. He was upset and
wanted someone to love. He went on a walk and
found a woman by herself. She decided to love him
and they both lived happily ever after.

JOELY BRADLEY (13)

Caldew School, Carlisle

TOO MUCH NOISE

It was time for my favourite TV programme but I could not hear it. The neighbour's baby was crying so I moved into the kitchen. Then I heard hammering so I moved into the bedroom and at last, peace and quiet but I'd missed my favourite programme!

BECKY POTTER (12)

Caldew School, Carlisle

17

MY HOLIDAY

One day I went on holiday and went for a walk with my dog in a forest. I fell down a big hole and I broke my leg. My dog ran away and I was screaming for an hour, I fainted and do not remember anything after that.

JACK HARRISON (12)

Caldew School, Carlisle

GUN

One day in London, a boy called Jay moved to a new estate. He was exploring a greenhouse; he lifted up a plant pot and found a gun! He was seen with the gun by a man called Jerry. Jerry took Jay to the station and Jay unluckily got sentenced.

BEN MONTGOMERY (12)

Caldew School, Carlisle

19

RACER

One day there was a boy called Jack, he wanted to race. Then it was his birthday, he got a motocross bike, he was so happy. He wanted to go on it and he did. Two days later he was in a race and he won first place!

CAMERON BRADLEY (12)

Caldew School, Carlisle

THE STRANGER

Fred went to play with his mates before the football
match started. His mum phoned him and
said, 'We're moving, get home.'
On the way home he met this man who
whispered, 'Do you want a lift?'
Fred said, 'No!'
Fred never got home, the man killed him.

BRENDAN TAYLOR (12)

Caldew School, Carlisle

THE FIND OF A STRANGER

'Come on James, we only have five
minutes left.' Harry said.
They were going to the park in the south of
Newcastle, the park was called Haythorn Park. Every
day they went to that park but this day there was
a very strange man sitting on the crooked old swing.

RYAN MITCHELL

Caldew School, Carlisle

IS HE ALIVE?

He found him down an alleyway, he was old and thin,
he looked lonely. He was wearing rags
and was smelly.
Billy ran home told his mum, dad and friends. They
all didn't believe him except for one person, an old
person, Hilda Rickerby. She asked him, 'Is he alive?'

SAMUEL SMITH (12)

Caldew School, Carlisle

THE SUMMER GARDEN

Slender water spirals down the glorious garden.
The fluffy grass flutters between my toes, just like the
butterflies flapping in the felt air. Nectar floats around
my nose cleansing my mind. The wise weeping
willow sways calmingly in the gentle breeze,
touching my ears. Tuneful birds whistle in the wind.

EMILY MECHIE (14)

Caldew School, Carlisle

JUST ANOTHER DAY

I'm brought to the ground with a *thud!* I try to push myself up with my hand but can't. Pain kicks in like a mini bomb exploding in my neck. I receive a jacket over me. The ambulance will be here soon I am told. Just another day.

WILLIAM TAYLOR (15)

Caldew School, Carlisle

DAYDREAM

I was sitting there all still, just listening, looking
around, daydreaming. This is how my day goes,
not doing anything, just here, a presence in the room,
amusing myself with a paper ball and two goals made
of pens. This is how school makes you, tired,
bored ... school's great!

MATTHEW FOSTER (15)

Caldew School, Carlisle

RED LASER

Ruler to the window, door ajar, hit the box,
red, yellow, blue. Join both wires, sparks fly, engine
going, sit down, belt up, look around. New wig,
nice shades, different jacket, luscious lips,
what's that noise?
Red laser on the ... *click, bang!*
Six foot under, flowers on me.

CHARLOTTE JAMES (14)

Caldew School, Carlisle

FRIENDLY FIRE

Friendly fire they said had done it, friendly fire! Not so friendly in my opinion. What friend would kill a friend? Death caused by opposition, OK but friends? His body to be returned by the week's end bringing with it depression and hate. One more brave man bites the dust.

SAM RICHARDS (15)

Caldew School, Carlisle

LITTLE RED AND THE WOLF

There once was a girl named Red whose grandma
had to stay in bed. She took her some cakes that
Little Red baked. When she got there her grandma
was dead! She found a big bad wolf in bed.
'What big teeth you have!'
'Better to eat you with!'

CLAIRE LITTLE (15)
Caldew School, Carlisle

CAT AND MOUSE

Her eyes jump wildly spying the scurrying victim.
She keeps her body flat to the ground, ears back and
eyes wide open. She creeps closer and closer, her
victim unaware. The long grass covers her slender
body as she settles down - it's only a matter of time
before she'll pounce …

CORINNE IRVING (14)

Caldew School, Carlisle

MY FIRST DAY

My first day at school, I thought it would be scary but I was wrong, it was amazing, other kids with me. The teacher was very kind, I thought everyone would be awful, they would pick on little kids like me, instead they were kind and helpful to us all.

ANNA DEWSNAP (15)

Caldew School, Carlisle

UNTITLED

There were a group of builders, they terrorised people. They went to a school and what a huge mistake. They put holes in walls, extra large pipes in random places and finally made as much noise as possible to beat their rival gang builders.

DANIEL PARK (14)

Caldew School, Carlisle

AS DEATH DAWNS

I began to fly. It was an unusual experience; I felt that
I could do anything. I am the sky, nothing can stick to
me, aeroplanes can fly through me, storms can pass
me but in the end I am still the sky and will
always be there.

SOPHIE KANE (15)
Caldew School, Carlisle

MY EX BEST FRIEND

She was my best friend; I could trust her with my life.
I could tell her anything in the world at all. We would
talk and talk for days on end. Chatting about football
or chatting about friends but then that all came to an
end, all over, never again.

FIONNTAN LAWLOR (15)

Caldew School, Carlisle

FRIENDS ARE FOREVER

It is so good to have friends, they can help you when you're low, share your secrets, but friends are for life not just to have for a day. So treat your friends with respect not like dirt on the bottom of your shoe. Best mates till the very end.

SOPHIE POTTER (12)

Caldew School, Carlisle

MY GARDEN

I was sunbathing in my garden when I heard someone shouting, 'Leave me alone! Get off me!' When I turned around there was no one in sight so I carried on sunbathing. When I woke up I was in a dark scary room. I shouted, 'Help! Where am I?'

ZOE THRELKELD (13)

Caldew School, Carlisle

BIG KICK

Scuba Steve went swimming when a shark bit his bum. Scuba Steve got really angry and hit him with his thumb. The shark got really scared and acted kind of weird. When Scuba Steve got home he decided to shave his beard!

JAMES BELL (15)

Caldew School, Carlisle

37

GROUNDED ON HOLIDAY

Great, we were going on holiday! It was the end of
the summer term at school. I was in Spain by the
pool when my sister started crying.
'You're grounded,' said my mum straight at me.
What did I do wrong? I have never, ever,
ever been grounded on holiday!

LAUREN CROFTS (13)
Caldew School, Carlisle

DON'T LOOK DOWN

Whack! I hit the jump at full speed. I was flying
through the air. I was red-hot with all my protection
on. My full face helmet was soaking wet then *boom!*
I hit the deck, my forks had bottomed out,
I'd nearly come off my bike. Good, I survived!

GRANT BRADDOCK (13)
Caldew School, Carlisle

SPORT HURTS

'And the bowler comes up and bowls it, *ouch!*
That must have hurt! Joe is rolling around on the
floor like a big girl. He would have been one if he did
not have a box on. Here comes an ambulance to
take Joe to the hospital.'

PHIL RICHARDSON (14)

Caldew School, Carlisle

TODAY IS A NEW DAY

Yesterday was the day of laughter, today is the day of
all days, it's Raise Money for Africa Day. Tomorrow is
a new day and we'll see tomorrow, why it's different
for today is more important. Last week was great,
this week's better. Who knows, next week
could be better.

ALEX CROOKS (14)

Caldew School, Carlisle

SNOWMAN

Snow glistening in the burning sun, snowmen with
their carrot noses and coal eyes. Motionless, standing
there like a lifeless person, frozen in an icy prison but
dressed with care. But soon this will all be gone,
all that will be left will be a puddle of water, no more.

RYAN WILKIE (13)

Caldew School, Carlisle

THE HOLOCAUST

I wait for them to leave and run to my mother and child and hide in a cupboard. We hear them coming and cry our eyes out. Then they stopped in the middle of the room. We held our breath in case they heard us but they left us alone.

BETH CARRICK (14)
Caldew School, Carlisle

PIRATES

Captain Prise stabbed Bill the pirate and Bill the
pirate said, 'My men will get you!'
Captain Prise had a peg leg and he had a sword with
a diamond on the end. His crew turned on him and
killed him and the crew were very rich.

STEPHEN KAVANAGH (11)

Caldew School, Carlisle

THE MAN

There is this garage where I live and in it there are
cobwebs, spiders, flies, furniture and … a man!
'What? There's a man in the garage?
What did he say?'
'What do I want? Have I got any Asprin?'
'What a weird man and he's in my own garage.
Wow!'

HANNAH STOBART (11)
Caldew School, Carlisle

TORTURER

My eyes slowly opened. As I tried to sit up,
something strong stopped me! Chains pulled me
down! Terror rushed down my body like I was in the
marathon. A figure stood in front of me! Something
made my eyes pop out. In the figure's hand
was an axe. 'Argh!'

NISHA HORSFIELD (12)

Caldew School, Carlisle

FANGS

I ran in terror and it followed me, its eyes glowing!
Running for my life I ran into the door! I lay still,
I could hear heavy breathing. I opened my eyes.
All I could see were huge fangs. I screamed! It ran off.
What was that big ugly creature?

ELENA SULLIVAN (12)
Caldew School, Carlisle

MURDER

I was walking through the wood and I heard
a scream. I ran back and someone had been
murdered so I ran back and I was shouting,
'Help! Help!' I went home and told my family that
someone had been murdered. I kept on shouting,
'Murder! Help!'

CHLOE RICHARDSON (13)

Caldew School, Carlisle

FRIENDS

It's good to have friends, especially when you're feeling down. Mates are great to listen to your secrets and you can always have a great laugh with them. Mates aren't for a day, they are for life.

REBECCA WATSON (13)
Caldew School, Carlisle

I AM A STAR

I look down on the Earth. I watch as days, seasons
and years go by. The moon shines down illuminating
our path. The sun shines bright as one hundred stars.
Black is all I see, I shine, I am a star.

HAZEL FURNISS (13)

Caldew School, Carlisle

CAKE

The lights dimmed and everyone looked really tense.
My heart pounded in my chest as the door creaked
open. Slowly a woman emerged holding something in
her hands. *Cake!* The crowd burst into song.
'Happy birthday to you!' they sung.
A smile appeared out of nowhere, ear to ear.

JAKE REED (12)

Caldew School, Carlisle

HORROR RIDE

The roller coaster went round and round, loop the
loop, left to right then down *crash! Bang! Wallop!*
It hit the ground. The screams echoed around the
theme park, crowds gathered in hundreds.
The whole place was silent for the very first time.
There were only three survivors!

JAYNE-ANN PINGUEY (13)

Caldew School, Carlisle

THE SLEEPOVER

One day, me, Jade and Amy were all staying at mine.
We all went on the trampoline; I showed them
the somersault on it.
Jade said, 'I will have a go at that,' and she fell
and broke her leg! She went to hospital.

JODIE CARTER (13)
Caldew School, Carlisle

ALONE AND SCARY

One lovely day as I walked to my nanna's house I felt an uncomfortable breeze down my back. As I turned around to investigate I screamed but it was just my imagination getting the better of me. So I turned around and walked nervously to my nanna's alone.

KIRSTY GRAHAM (13)

Caldew School, Carlisle

THE GODZILLA STORY

Once upon a time there was a monster called Godzilla. He lived in China on top of a volcano. He was happy because he lived on top of the volcano. One day he was bored so he went down to China to kill lots of people.

DAVID HICKSON (14)
Caldew School, Carlisle

UNTITLED

I open the door. I hear noises; I walk on, cobwebs
brush against my face. There is lots of rubbish and
newspapers. I see something in the corner.
I move towards it. I get up close and see what it is.
It is a man!
'What do you want?'

BEN ARMSTRONG (11)
Caldew School, Carlisle

CHOCOLATE

Smooth, dark and hard with a rich smell, milk, white and plain with fruit or biscuit as extras, covered in a shiny wrapper. Cadburys, Galaxy Nestle and Thorntons. *Yum-yum!* I love them all. Can also be ice cream or even a hot drink. Chocolate is popular, especially at Easter.

SARAH WILSON (13)

Caldew School, Carlisle

CREATURES OF THE MIST

The warriors stood among the burnt demolished
village waiting for the creatures to come. They were
tired and weary from the countless attacks. The
creatures attacked them. They knew this would be
the last fight. They waited, swords in hands, then
they heard it, the horn bellowed, they were coming!

RHYS PATTISON (13)

Caldew School, Carlisle

THE SHADOWS

'The shadows have got me!' she said, 'send backup
to ...' It crackled off.
I was the last survivor of the massacre. But why,
why was someone holding my hand? When I turned
around there he was, the shadow man! I tried to
raise my fist ... then I woke up.

MATTHEW BURNS (13)
Caldew School, Carlisle

HAUNTED HOUSE

I walked into a haunted house. It was scary.
I went to look for my friends. I heard a scream and
went upstairs. I walked into a bedroom. There was
a monster! It tried to eat me! I ran as fast as I could,
I got out, I was safe!

NATHAN PILMER (13)

Caldew School, Carlisle

THE ZOO ESCAPE

Today I went on a trip to the zoo. When I got there some animals had escaped. There were animals running around everywhere and animal keepers too. A few hours later the animals had been put back in their living places but the tiger hadn't been found ...

KATHERINE NELSON (13)

Caldew School, Carlisle

THE TREASURE HUNT

We went into the tomb. We were looking for ancient treasure, we were right at the bottom then we found it, the treasure chest! There were skeletons all over the room where they had been killed trying to get the treasure. I got in! It was a huge diamond!

KARL DIXON (14)

St Benedict's Catholic High School, Whitehaven

THERE WAS HOPE!

Traipsing through the sticky humid heat of the
Quarliki Rainforest, I wondered if I'd ever find it.
I'd been walking for days but to me it felt like years.
Then, as I pushed back the leaves, there it was!
I'd finally found it! There was hope at last in sight.

BETHANY PINK (14)
St Benedict's Catholic High School, Whitehaven

A NEW WORLD

The sharpness of the red water hit me like a ton of bricks. The waterfall poured magnificently around me like a stream of gold. I felt a bitter-sweet sensation like never before as I glided through the glimmering waterfall. The tips of my bewildered toes entered a new world.

AIMEE BAWDEN (14)
St Benedict's Catholic High School, Whitehaven

TUNNEL

How did we get this far down, this tunnel is so deep,
it goes past the dinosaurs' graves. It goes deep down
underground. If we keep going we might end up in
Australia. Well, slight exaggeration, it was a small
tunnel in the back garden that the dog had dug.

KAYLEIGH MOYNES (14)
St Benedict's Catholic High School, Whitehaven

WHAT IS THIS THING?

How did we ever get this high? What is that in the
distance? Is it what we have been looking for?
Oh no, it's only a satellite! But wait, what is this on
the horizon? Could this be … yes! Yes it is,
it's a UFO! Help, it's drawing me in!

BRAD LOFTHOUSE (14)

St Benedict's Catholic High School, Whitehaven

A DINNERTIME TO REMEMBER

Sharp pain was running through my head, pulling on my scalp. Pain wasn't even the word. Everything was all fuzzy, what happened that dinnertime I'll never forget. *Snip! Snip!* It was all falling to the floor. 'Oh no!' The bubblegum from my hair had to be cut out! '

STEFANIE MCCABE (14)
St Benedict's Catholic High School, Whitehaven

67

IS IT A BLACK HOLE?

I stumbled over the big obstacles lying on the dark, damp floor. I felt like I was falling into a black hole and was going to be lost forever. My heart was racing, palms sweating. Who knew that getting childhood photos from the attic would be so heart bursting.

BROGAN GREEN (13)
St Benedict's Catholic High School, Whitehaven

WOW!

Looking around me it was so big, there were so many people. I knew that it was going to be the best. Up and down, round and round it went, it looked terrifying I knew that if I didn't go on this ride I would regret it.

MAHMUDA BEGUM (14)

St Benedict's Catholic High School, Whitehaven

69

MIDNIGHT MURDER

As Adam was walking down an alley he stopped and looked, he could see a white and red hoody heading towards him. He continued walking, he was two feet away. He clipped him, dragged him to his van. He shouted but no one heard him!
He was shot five times!

JOSH JENKINSON (13)
St Benedict's Catholic High School, Whitehaven

THE JOURNEY

I wait for a while. I walk up the stairs and pay my
amount. I look up and millions of eyes are watching
down the aisle I walk. I feel the breath on my back.
Here I get off, I hate travelling by bus.

KYLE HANNAH (14)
St Benedict's Catholic High School, Whitehaven

THE TRAIN ROBBERY

The sun was beating down, the horses going full pace alongside the train. From the back of the carriage, the wannabe cowboys strutted through the aisles. The people, terrified, handed over anything and everything. Satisfied with their loot the highwaymen jumped off the train, riding into the sunset.

OLIVIA MASON (14)
St Benedict's Catholic High School, Whitehaven

MY MUMMY

A mummy all scary and frightening, I scream for help.
Argh! Nobody hears. It gets closer, its arms stretched
out. I back into a corner, I'm trapped!
I can feel its breath on my neck as it says, 'Come on,
give me a hug.'
'No, Mam, I won't!'

ANDREW BEERES (14)
St Benedict's Catholic High School, Whitehaven

THE LAST CORNER

Coming up on the last corner, Speed Demon,
The King and Fly High are all in a line. Suddenly
they crash into each other, all three topple, all three
drivers fly out and slide across the track. The one to
cross the line is The King. The King's the champ.

JACK STAINTON (14)

St Benedict's Catholic High School, Whitehaven

LEFT IN THE DARK

It's bedtime, the thing I hate. I shut my door and run and jump in bed just in case he gets me! I lie in bed awake, left in the dark. I can't sleep just in case the monster pops up from under my bed and eats me!

SARAH ROONEY (14)
St Benedict's Catholic High School, Whitehaven

75

CUSTOMER SERVICE

A man barged to the front of a queue at Heathrow
airport, the woman wouldn't serve him and he
started yelling 'Do you know who I am?'
The woman grabbed the microphone and said,
'We have a passenger here who doesn't know who
he is, can anyone help?'

DANIELLE MCGARRY (14)
St Benedict's Catholic High School, Whitehaven

THE OGRE

I walked in to the dark house and sitting there was the monster ogre. He slowly stepped towards me and attacked me vigorously. But then I woke up and my dog was chewing my leg!

GREGG CUNNINGHAM (14)

St Benedict's Catholic High School, Whitehaven

SMILES

She never smiles, ever! Well, after her mum you can't
blame her. Remember the cancer? She's never set
foot in a hospital since. Poor kid, only twelve,
you think she knew? And that's why, what a thing
for a child to have to go through.

KATHERINE LENNOX (14)

St Benedict's Catholic High School, Whitehaven

UNTITLED

I stepped up to the platform; I felt the pressure of hundreds of eyes watching me. Sweat trickled down my brow and caressed my dry lips as I waited for judgement. The room was silent as the judge's hammer swung down and called '10!'
Phew! I hate weighing day!

SAM MASON (14)
St Benedict's Catholic High School, Whitehaven

THE GREAT OUTDOORS

Hacking my way through the towering trees and
branches, nettles prickling my skin as I searched.
A sudden noise from behind made me jump.
Losing my balance, I toppled to the ground.
He came towards me. *Bark!* 'Sparky?'
This garden had completely turned into
a jungle … now where's that frisbee?

TANIA HOQUE (14)
St Benedict's Catholic High School, Whitehaven

ROOM OF DESPAIR

I stumbled into the dark cold room. The stench was
terrible. My eyes adjusted to the dark at the far end
of the room, I saw what looked like a bed.
I wish I had listened to my mum when she said
clean your bedroom Rory, why didn't I?

RORY WILSON (13)
St Benedict's Catholic High School, Whitehaven

SNOW WHITE AND THE SEVEN VERTICALLY CHALLENGED MEN

Snow White and the seven vertically challenged people were visiting Whitehaven. It had hit the local news. Unfortunately she didn't know someone was after her. The assassin fired his gun. Suddenly Grumpy jumped in front of the bullet and he's Grumpy no more!

ALEX CANAVAN (14)

St Benedict's Catholic High School, Whitehaven

THE GAP

I pressed down on the pedal and the throttle opened
fully. I saw the gap; it was small and closing fast.
I was picking up speed, 200mph, 210mph, 220mph!
I sped forward as the gap between the cars closed.
I was through, the chequered flag for me!

LUKE BOUNDS (14)

St Benedict's Catholic High School, Whitehaven

THE KICK

The tension is building up. My foot could be the hero
for my queen and country. This has to be the best
kick of my life so far. It needs power to have a chance
to pass the keeper. I step back gingerly,
slowly and nervously I run and shoot.

CRAIG SMITH (14)

St Benedict's Catholic High School, Whitehaven

THE EXPERIMENT

My hands trembled, cold shivers ran back and forth
down my spine. It sat deadly still on the floor in front
of me. I walked over the bottle tightly secured in my
hand. I threw the bottle and dived to the floor.
I sat shielded, *bang!* What had I done?

REBECCA SOUTHWARD (14)

St Benedict's Catholic High School, Whitehaven

MY DESTINATION

Bang! I slammed the car door shut. I slowly shuffled
along the path to the sharp pointed gate. I stopped,
I froze. I didn't want to go but I knew I had to.
I scanned the area, no sight of any human beings,
I had reached my destination … school!

HOLLY SLOAN (14)

St Benedict's Catholic High School, Whitehaven

WAITING

I waited, just sitting there in the dark. Waiting,
thoughts crept into my head, thoughts of death and
loneliness, thoughts of hunger and pain. The darkness
was slowly seeping all around me, waiting for
a chance to consume my soul, turning me into
another mindless robot. Silent, alone, waiting.

TIM BUTLER (14)
St Benedict's Catholic High School, Whitehaven

THE GIG

The heat forced me to sleep but I fought. I had to stay standing, the people swallowing me. I ploughed on, lights, I ran, pushing past, curling my fingers round the metal railing but the heat pulled me away. I drifted backwards, he grabbed me, he saved me, the singer!

KIM SOPPITT (14)
St Benedict's Catholic High School, Whitehaven

TRAPPED

Bang! The heavy door slammed. I wandered upstairs.
In the bedroom everything was covered with cloths.
No one had been here for years. Footsteps were
getting closer. Who was it? *Bang* on the door.
I turned even though I knew I shouldn't.
How was I going to escape?

HEATHER WARD (14)

St Benedict's Catholic High School, Whitehaven

MY TURN

I couldn't stand still. I was so excited! Why was it taking so long? Finally, just one minute more to wait, it seemed to last for hours. I was growing more impatient. At last my turn! I got strapped in, my heart in my mouth. The roller coaster flew off.

CATHERINE CAMPBELL (14)
St Benedict's Catholic High School, Whitehaven

DISTURBIA

Forbidden is not the word. Eerie sounds more like it. Enchanted, disintegrated, melancholic, decrepit, brooding, all spring to mind. A chill creeps up my spine and creeps back down again. The rusty gate screeches open. My heart beats louder and louder pounding out of my chest. Dare I enter?

JAMIE~MARIE FOX (13)
St Benedict's Catholic High School, Whitehaven

91

SPIDERS, SPIDERS EVERYWHERE

Once when shopping in Hawkins Bazaar,
I was playing with a remote-controlled giant spider.
A boy came in and saw the spider moving but didn't
see me with the control. So scared, he ran out crying
with his mum. He had thought it was a real spider!

ALICE MCDONALD (12)

William Howard School, Brampton

MY PAINFUL JOURNEY

One day I was playing on my trampoline, happy and cheerful, my friends were there. I jumped as high as possible while my friends screamed, 'Be careful.'
But it was too late. I flew up in the air and smashed into a tree.
'Ouch!' I cried then I was unconscious.

NEIL LITTLE (12)
William Howard School, Brampton

MY FIRST ASTHMA ATTACK

Foreign currency, suitcases and teddy, everything
packed ready for the off. Excitement everywhere
but one thing wasn't right. My first asthma attack
ended our holiday before it started. Transport was
ambulance not aeroplane. Destination was hospital
not Portugal. Oxygen masks and steroids
were my only hope.

MELISSA WRIGHT (12)

William Howard School, Brampton

UNTITLED

I was jumping with my pony in the field, a sudden *bang* went off. My pony startled and galloped off. He launched himself over the five-bar gate. I didn't have time to scream. Suddenly, I wished that I hadn't been teaching him to jump the gate into the field!

SARAH JORDAN (12)
William Howard School, Brampton

THE CHEESE OBSESSION

I used to be a normal boy until it came to me, the
Cheddar, the mozzarella. My obsession was cheese.
First the books, then even more extreme, a book
talk. This obsession with cheese will never end.
The books pile in all the information.
One day I know I'll explode!

NATHANIEL GUNTER (12)

William Howard School, Brampton

THE SPY

In the cold black night in the London mist, the spy was ready to grab the girl. He had been waiting three hours. They took her to their secret underground base on Guernsey. They glued plastic explosives to her and returned her with a note attached.
'£2,000,000 or death, ha!'

MATT ROBERTS (12)
William Howard School, Brampton

97

THE TROUBLE WITH BEING TALL

Lots of people think being tall is great but it isn't.
Mind you, being tall is how I got out of school. People
said to me, 'Get that tennis ball off the roof.'
So I did. My big hands slipped through the roof,
the roof landed on a teacher, *oops!*

DARRELL BURNET (12)

William Howard School, Brampton

AMY'S FRIGHT SCENE

The street Amy had to walk down was dark, cold and wet, stray cats were following her. She was all alone, her spine tingled and she shuddered at the sight of a bat swooping above her. She was terrified. 'And cut, that's a wrap. Okay everyone, take a break.'

AILSA MCALISTER (12)
William Howard School, Brampton

THE FOLLOWER

I knew someone was following me. I could hear the creaking behind. I started to sweat. I was feeling weaker and weaker. It was getting louder and louder the thing behind me. I knew it was there, I decided to face it but to my dismay it was a dog!

HOLLY COSGROVE (12)

William Howard School, Brampton

AHH!

Beads of sweat trickle down my face, I grip the ropes tightly and throw myself forwards. I'm going higher and higher. I let go and I'm falling, down, down and *splash!* I hit the water with the force of a freight train and I'm hurled down river. Stupid swing!

HENRY GRAINGER (12)
William Howard School, Brampton

POP STAR SPELL

'Yibbery fibbery zing zang zoo, I want to be a pop
star la, la, la.' I add some tone and a cool song.
I say 'Hocus pocus'
It goes *bang* in a puff of smoke, I'm a singing star.
I start to sing but all I say is 'Blah, blah!'

ANNIE HARDING (12)

William Howard School, Brampton

THE BULLY

I got off my school bus and a bully pushed me so
I pushed him back and told him to go away so I went
and met Alex outside school. The bully walked
past and tripped me up. This incident sent me to
hospital with brain damage.

AARON THORPE (12)
William Howard School, Brampton

THE SEASIDE

Yummy! Happily I ran down the beach to Mum.
Yum! Ice cream! *Splash!* Fun in the sun. *Ouch!*
Sunburn, slap on the suncream. Sugar sweets,
what a good day.

JILL VEVERS (11)

William Howard School, Brampton

SUMMER ON A FARM

I live on a farm. I like it when they cut the grass.
I sometimes get to ride in the tractors and
sometimes the chopper. We have to shut our dogs in
because they get in the way. There is lots of grass to
feed the cows and the sheep.

DAWN IRELAND (12)

William Howard School, Brampton

THE DENTIST

The knife glinted in the harsh light, drawing ever
closer. A metallic whirring started and a creature
with no mouth loomed over, blinding me
with white light.
'Well, it looks alright but a filling may be needed
in a few months.'
I had survived the dentist!

ANNA YOUNG (12)
William Howard School, Brampton

INFORMATION

We hope you have enjoyed reading this book - and that you will
continue to enjoy it in the coming years.

If you like reading and writing, drop us a line or give us a call and we'll
send you a free information pack. Alternatively visit our website at
www.youngwriters.co.uk

Write to:
Young Writers Information,
Remus House,
Coltsfoot Drive,
Peterborough,
PE2 9JX

Tel: (01733) 890066
Email: youngwriters@forwardpress.co.uk